The Dinosaur Museum

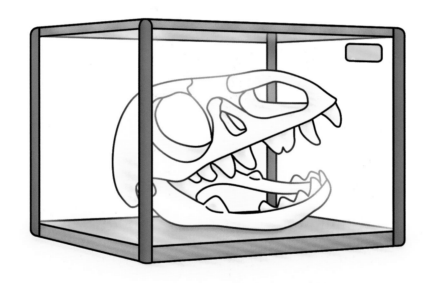

Adaptation from the animated series: Anne Paradis
Illustrations taken from the animated series and adapted by Mario Allard

Caillou and his family are going to the museum to see the dinosaurs. Caillou loves dinosaurs. His favorite stuffed animal, Rexy, is a dinosaur. Just as they're about to leave, Caillou says, "I forgot Rexy. I can't go to the dinosaur museum without him." Caillou runs back into the house to get Rexy.

While Mommy is buying the tickets, Caillou asks why there are no more dinosaurs on Earth.

"Nobody knows for sure," Daddy tells him. "Some people think it got too cold for them, and other people think that a giant meteorite hit the Earth."

Mommy comes back with the tickets. Caillou puts Rexy down to take his ticket, then runs to the museum entrance.

"Caillou!" Mommy calls. "Aren't you forgetting someone?"
Caillou comes back and sees Rexy on the ground. He picks
his dinosaur up and hugs him.
"Would you like to leave Rexy in the car?" Mommy asks.
"He'll be safe there."
"I'll keep him with me the whole time," Caillou promises.

Caillou wonders why the dinosaurs don't have any skin.
"The only thing left of the dinosaurs is their bones. When researchers found them, they had to put them back together like a puzzle. That's how we know what dinosaurs looked like, Mommy explained."

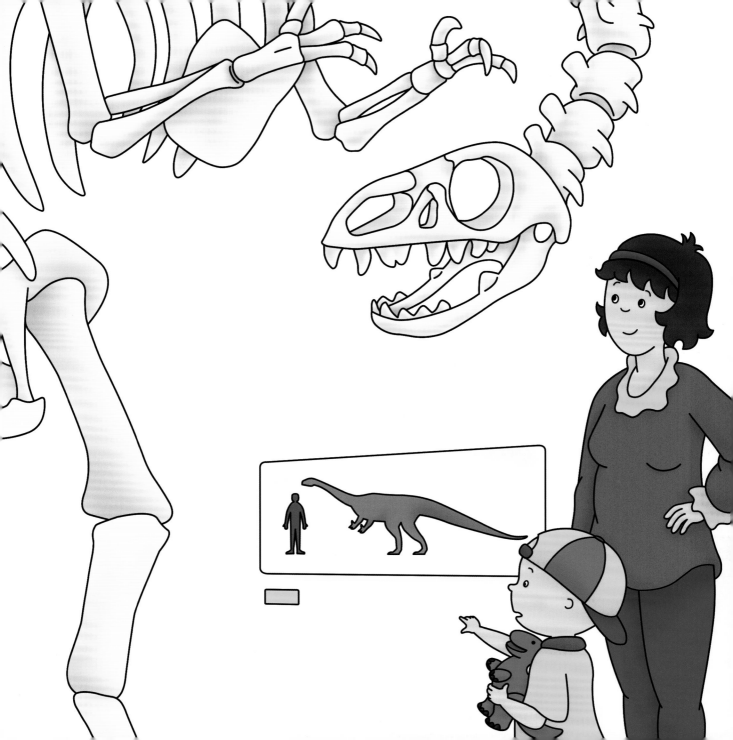

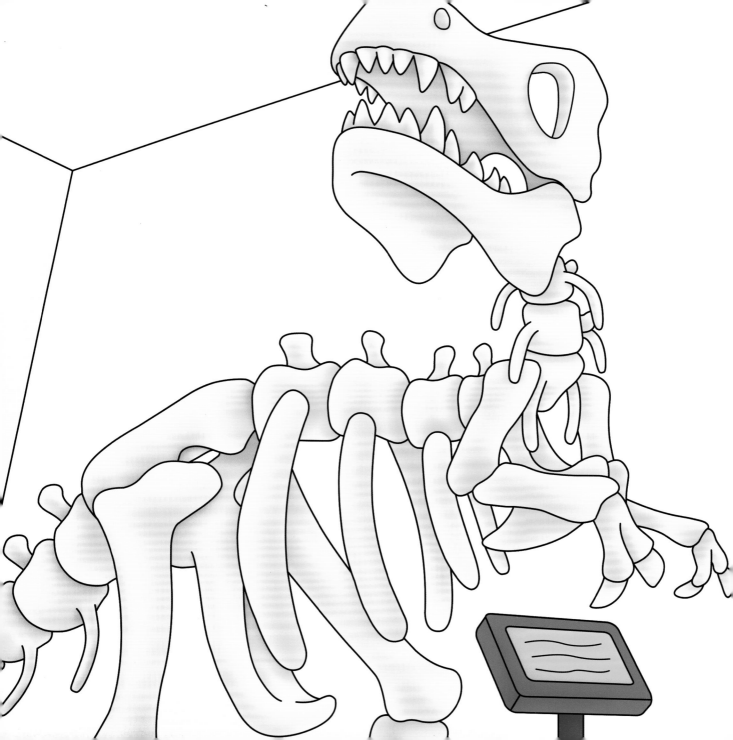

Mommy and Caillou look at another skeleton.
"These are the bones of a T. rex. He belongs
to the same species as your dinosaur," Mommy says.
Caillou is astonished. "Look how big he is!"
"Rexy!" Rosie cries.

"Look, it's a flying dinosaur!" Caillou exclaims.
"That's a pterodactyl," Daddy says.
Caillou had no idea there were so many kinds of dinosaurs.
He is trying to imagine what life would have been like in
the time of the dinosaurs.

When Caillou stops daydreaming, he can't see his family anymore. Caillou decides that he'd better stay right where he is. That's what Mommy told him to do if he ever got lost. A museum guard says to him, "Hi there, buddy. Why are you all by yourself?" Caillou isn't supposed to talk to strangers, but he knows he can talk to people who work at the museum.

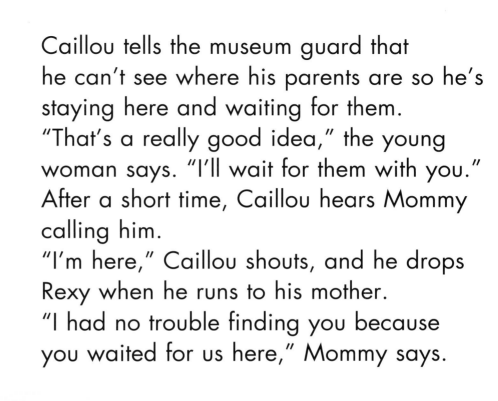

Caillou tells the museum guard that he can't see where his parents are so he's staying here and waiting for them.
"That's a really good idea," the young woman says. "I'll wait for them with you."
After a short time, Caillou hears Mommy calling him.
"I'm here," Caillou shouts, and he drops Rexy when he runs to his mother.
"I had no trouble finding you because you waited for us here," Mommy says.

Caillou and his family end their visit with in the hall of the woolly mammoth, ancestor of the elephants.

"So Caillou, did you enjoy the museum?" Mommy asks.

"Oh, yes! Caillou answers.

"Now you know what Rexy's family looks like."

"Oh, no—Rexy! I lost him, says Caillou."

Daddy and Caillou go to the lost and found.
"If someone found Rexy, they might have brought him here," Daddy explains.
But Rexy isn't there.

Daddy and Caillou retrace their steps to see if they can find Rexy.
In the hall where he got lost, Caillou sees the guard holding a dinosaur. It's Rexy!
The guard says, "Your dinosaur waited patiently, just like you."

When they go back to the exit, Caillou runs to Mommy.
"We found Rexy!"
"Did you have trouble finding him?" Mommy asks.
"No, because he stayed where he was, the way I told him to."
"Rexy's a very smart little dinosaur," Mommy says.
"Way to go, Rexy!" Caillou says, and hugs him.

Text: adaptation by Anne Paradis of the animated series CAILLOU,
produced by DHX Media Inc.
All rights reserved.
Translation: Joann Egar
Original story: Nisha Muire
Original Episode #274: The Dinosaur Hunter
Illustrations: Mario Allard, based on the animated series CAILLOU
Coloration: Eric Lehouillier

The PBS KIDS logo is a registered mark of PBS and is used with permission.

Chouette Publishing would like to thank the Government of Canada and SODEC
for their financial support.

Bibliothèque et Archives nationales du Québec and Library and Archives
Canada cataloguing in publication

Paradis, Anne, 1972-

[Sur la trace des dinosaures. English]

The dinosaur museum/adaptation, Anne Paradis; illustrations, Mario Allard;
translation, Joann Egar.

(Caillou)
(Clubhouse)
Translation of: Sur la trace des dinosaures.
Target audience: For children aged 3 and up.

ISBN 978-2-89718-518-3 (softcover)

1. Caillou (Fictitious character) - Juvenile literature. 2. Dinosaurs - Juvenile literature.
I. Allard, Mario, 1969-, illustrator. II. Egar, Joann, translator. III. Title. IV. Title: Sur
la trace des dinosaures. English. V. Series: Caillou. VI. Series: Clubhouse.

QE861.5.P3713 2019   j567.9   C2018-942626-8

Printed in China
10 9 8 7 6 5 4 3 2 1 CHO2047 NOV2018

INCH AND ROLY

and the Sunny Day Scare

by Melissa Wiley
illustrated by Ag Jatkowska

READY-TO-READ

Simon Spotlight

New York London Toronto Sydney New Delhi

For my goddaughter, Vivienne
—M. W.

For Michal and Eddie, for bringing the
sunshine to my life
—A. J.

 SIMON SPOTLIGHT
An imprint of Simon & Schuster Children's Publishing Division
1230 Avenue of the Americas, New York, New York 10020
Text copyright © 2014 by Melissa Anne Peterson
Illustrations copyright © 2014 by Ag Jatkowska
SIMON SPOTLIGHT, READY-TO-READ, and colophon are registered trademarks of Simon & Schuster, Inc
For information about special discounts for bulk purchases, please contact Simon & Schuster Special Sales
at 1-866-506-1949 or business@simonandschuster.com.
The Simon & Schuster Speakers Bureau can bring authors to your live event. For more information or to
book an event contact the Simon & Schuster Speakers Bureau at 1-866-248-3049 or visit our website at
www.simonspeakers.com.
Manufactured in the United States of America 0314 LAK
First Edition 10 9 8 7 6 5 4 3 2 1
Library of Congress Cataloging-in-Publication Data
Wiley, Melissa.
Inch and Roly and the sunny day scare / by Melissa Wiley ; illustrated by Ag Jatkowska. — First edition.
pages cm. — (Ready-to-read)
Summary: Roly and her friends try to identify an object she finds in the grass, but from their different
perspectives it could be a tunnel, a hill, or even a snake.
[1. Insects—Fiction. 2. Worms—Fiction.] I. Jatkowska, Ag, illustrator. II. Title.
PZ7.W64814Imm 2014
[E]—dc23
2013010915
ISBN 978-1-4424-9071-0 (pbk)
ISBN 978-1-4424-9072-7 (hc)
ISBN 978-1-4424-9073-4 (eBook)

Roly Poly saw a strange thing  in the grass.

"What is this thing?"
Roly asked.
Inchworm took a look.
He saw a dark hole.

It is a tunnel," said Inch.

"It is a dark tunnel
that drips."

"Let me see," said Beetle.
Beetle looked at the thing.

"It is not a tunnel,"
she said.

"It is a nice green hill."

"Let me see,"
said Dragonfly.
Dragonfly flew up high
and looked down.

"It is not a hill!"
he yelled.
"It is a snake!
It is a big, scary snake!"

"A snake?" asked Beetle.

"Yikes!" said Inch.

"Run!" yelled Beetle.

"Fly!" cried Dragonfly.

"I cannot fly!"
cried Inch.

"Then flee!" فرارکی سے yelled Dragonfly.

"Wait!" cried Roly.
"Do not flee.
Do not fly."

Beetle stopped running.

Dragonfly stopped flying.

Inch stopped fleeing.

They all looked at Roly.

"A thing cannot be a tunnel, بودن

and a hill,

and a snake," said Roly.

"It must be something else." دیگران

Roly peeked in the tunnel.

She climbed over the hill.

She rolled along the back
of the snake.

"I know what this thing is," said Roly. "This thing is a hose!"

"A hose?" asked Dragonfly.
"That is not scary,"
said Inch.

"That is a good thing," said Beetle.

"Yes," said Roly.

"A hose is a very good thing
when you need a drink.

چه زمانی

And after all this yelling,

بعد از

I am very thirsty!"